Bobby Bear
and The
Magical Bamboo Forest

Written and Illustrated
By
John W. Howard II

To order additional copies of this book, contact:
Xlibris
1-888-795-4274
www.Xlibris.com
Orders@Xlibris.com

Bobby Bear is a very unique and special bear.

Bobby lives in his own secret cave and loves to read and use his computer. He loves history and mystery books. Bobby has always been a bear of adventure. Bobby loves to garden, go hiking and fishing. Bobby has even entered a marathon, but what Bobby likes to do, most of all is eat bamboo.

One day while Bobby was gardening he found a map. Bobby loves geography and likes to study about far-away lands. Well, Bobby had an idea that this map was a secret map to the **Magical Bamboo Forest.** Bobby had heard about this forest in legends and through stories that his father used to tell him when he was younger, but he really did not know whether it really existed.

Bobby made up his mind: he was going to find this *Magical Bamboo Forest.* He packed up his supplies for his long journey and even asked for advice and support from his friends. To Bobby's surprise his friends said that he was crazy and very foolish for ever thinking of such an idea. They said that he was in a wheelchair and would never be able to make it.

Bobby just laughed at their lack of confidence in him, remembering that they said the same things to him when he wanted to enter a marathon and headed out on his way. He first had to cross the desert. It was very hot, and Bobby noticed strange birds always following him. They never spoke and kept drooling when they looked at him.

The buzzards left Bobby alone, quite surprised to see him make it through the desert. Bobby looked at his map once more to make sure he was going the right way and found it getting quite cold.

Bobby noticed that there was snow and ice around. He had seen snow and ice before, but not like this. Then all of a sudden he saw a group of animals who looked something like him; they had the same colors, but there was something different.
Bobby went over to them anyway, introduced himself and asked about this strange new place. Well these animals called themselves penguins and laughed and made fun of Bobby, saying that he looked funny and couldn't walk. This made Bobby very angry. Bobby explained to the penguins that the things which they said were rude and very mean. He also explained to the penguins that he is a bear, and bears can eat penguins regardless of whether they can walk.

Realizing that bobby meant business, the penguins apologized. Bobby explained to them that he was an animal too and deserved the same respect that they would give other animals. They were very respectful of Bobby's quest for the *Magical Bamboo Forest* and helped him by giving him some fish to eat and guided him in the right direction to continue his journey.

After making friends with the penguins and thanking them for their help, Bobby met a new challenge; mountains. The mountains were tough to climb. It was steep with many loose rocks, making it hard for the wheels on Bobby's chair to move. Bobby was the only one up there except for a mountain goat, but he was too far away for Bobby to even say hello.

Bobby finally made it over the mountains. He was now at the ocean. Bobby was excited that he had made it this far, but he faced a big problem. How was he going to get across the ocean? Bobby could swim, but the ocean was very big. And besides, how was he going to get his wheelchair across? Bobby was upset. He thought his journey was going to end right there. After all that effort, he would be stopped because he did not have a way across the ocean. Just at that moment a whale noticed Bobby at the shore and went closer to see what was going on. He had heard Bobby's cries all the way under the water. Bobby told the great whale of his journey and that it meant a lot to him to get to the **Magical Bamboo Forest.** Well, the whale was very impressed by Bobby's courage and insisted on giving Bobby a ride to the other side of the ocean.

Bobby was grateful for what the great whale had done for him, but Bobby was sad that he could not do something for the whale. The whale explained to Bobby that it is important for him to succeed in his goal, and that if Bobby does that, which is how he could show thanks. The great whale knew that Bobby had a good heart and would have done the same for him. Bobby gave the great whale a big hug and continued on his journey.

Bobby really liked the great whale because he believed in Bobby and respected him for who he was. This encouragement from the great whale made Bobby excited and he started to move faster. He somehow knew that he was getting closer to the end of his long journey.

Then; there it was, the Mystical, *Magical, Bamboo Forest.* This is the forest that he had heard about in stories as a child. *It was beautiful!* There was bamboo everywhere, and it seemed as though the forest welcomed him. There was plenty to eat, and the sun brightly shinned through the forest. Bobby decided to construct a monument in the center of the forest out of respect for those animals who helped him, and to remember those animals that never had a chance. Bobby's dream and goal is much like our own. We all can succeed no matted what the odds are. We just have to have faith and allowed a chance . . . .

. . . .

Printed in the United States
By Bookmasters